all rights reserved
CIP data is available
published in
the united states 2007
by blue apple books
515 valley street
maplewood, n.j. 07040
www.blueapplebooks.com
distributed in the u.s.
by chronicle books
first edition
printed in china
ISBN 13: 978-1-59354-596-3
ISBN 10: 1-59354-596-7

13 5 7 9 10 8 6 4 2

what are these numbers for, anyway?

dedicated
with love to
lene
stefan
pierre
kirsten
chip, and
my
DADDY
I PINCH YOUR CLAWS!

text and illustrations copyright ©

2007

| by laurie rosenwald
no cutting and pasting!
also, do not dunk in
HOT CHICKEN FAT!

and to name but just a few:

RED

yellow

GREEN BLUE

written and

illustrated by

BLUE APPLE

laurie rosenwald

KETCHUP ON YOUR FRIES

cherries in your pies planet MARS in space

lipstick on your face

LOBSTERS
for
your
lunch

ROSES
in
a
bunch

STOP was that a **SIGN?**

CALL on the **HOT**LINE!

FIRE TRUCK

AHEAD

all of them are

RED

jeans **are** blue

blue jays
are too

mailboxes
to send your MAIL

**and
a** shark
who has a **tail**

the sky is BLUE

the ocean's BLUE

and if you're sad YOU could be BLUE

with his big blue eyes
he cries and cries and cries!

do you have a **bright blue** suit?

do you have a small blue FRUIT?

blues are just the song to sing when you don't have **anything!**

HERE, HAVE A MINT!

GREEN

IS THE TINT.

lettuce
explain:

olives
trees

pickles
peas.

*this
inchworm
doesn't
rhyme
with
anything!

*

but don't
eat it,
please,
If you
find it
on

cheese.

if you're jealous and angry that **you** can't be **me,**
they might call this mood you're in

GREEN with

EN-VY!

is my NAME.
i can be a
flame!

or the
setting
sun

when the night's begun.

NGE

redheads? really orange. goldfish? orange too.

CARROTS are this color. WAIT! there is another! something good to eat, and it's rather sweet…and i kind of feel, that it has a PEEL…

you

ora

guessed it! an

nge!

what a fruit!
wow

landed
on my
FAVORITE
knee
and
i got a
PURPLE
BRUISE!

sun-
shine,
LEMONS,
and
a
YOLK!

grass

finger paint

spinach

➡ lime

icky

bluey

olive

mixed with **blue**
i will be **green**
or with **red**

an

ORANGE

scene!

V-8 | fanta | tangerine | taxi | mod

LEMON YELLOW
Jaune Citron
Zitronengelb
Amarillo Limón
Giallo Limone

WINSOR & NEWTON
DESIGNERS
GOUACHE

HORADAM GOUACHE
864 AERO finest ①
Ultramarine deep
Ultramarin dunkel
ultramarine deep
outremer foncé
ultramar oscuro

just because they're wearing silly pink **tutus,** even if they've bought some **pretty pink toe shoes,** they're **no ballerinas,** they're just **flamingooos!**

IF you want to make some trouble go ahead and **blow** a

WHETHER **you are old or young,** doctors say, **"STICK OUT YOUR TONGUE!"**

Bubble

crossword puzzles
and their
clues

READ THEM IN THE MORNING NEWS

just like
yellows, reds, and blues...

BLACK

AND WHITE

ARE colors TOO!

i can
think of
MORE......

can
YOU?

JAN 1 0 2008

blueberry pie

turquoise

cobalt

i'm not sure

nothing

regular blue